THE QUIET KOALA

FROM WALLA WALLA

By Wally Bee

To my parents,
thank you both for helping
me with my shyness.

There once was a quiet koala,
who came from the town Walla Walla.

As much as she'd try, she was so very shy,
when classmates asked "Why?,"
she just wanted to cry.

One day the teacher announced just after the bell.
All the children were going to do show and tell.

I can't speak to the class thought the little koala.
I really don't wanna!

She talked to her parents later that day
and they said, "Don't dwell"
And then her Mom said, "You will really be
swell."

The koala thought she could make them see why.
But on the other claw, maybe she could give it a try.

Show and tell started with young Iggy the Iguana.
She told everyone about her Abuela in Guatemala.

The quiet Koala let out a long sigh. Iggy's show and tell looked just as easy as pie.

The koala was feeling under a spell,
And did not seem too ready to do show
and tell.

The teacher said, "Better start, do not delay,
I'll bet that you have some great things to say."

The quiet koala took a breath and stood tall,
And smiled at the class and said to them all,

"I may be a koala who's from Walla Walla, But my name is Mahalia and I was born in Australia."

The End

About The Author

Since an early age, Wally Bee loved to draw and create characters. After working in the publishing industry for over a decade, he is finally bringing his characters to life. Wally wants to tell stories that help very young children understand the world around them. "I Am", his first children's book, was written for his first son and can be appreciated by all little ones. "The Quiet Koala from Walla Walla" is his second book and aims to provide inspiration for shy kids. In his spare time, Wally Bee scribbles enthusiastically in his notebooks searching for the best way to tell his next story. He currently lives with his wife and two sons outside New York City.

CPSIA information can be obtained
at www.ICGtesting.com
Printed in the USA
LVHW071156160723
752563LV00019B/5